Kitten Campout

Swim into more adventures!

PuRRmaiDS

The Scaredy Cat
The Catfish Club
Seasick Sea Horse
Search for the Mermicorn
A Star Purr-formance
Quest for Clean Water
Kittens in the Kitchen
Merry Fish-mas

MeRmicoRnS

Sparkle Magic
A Friendship Problem

PuRRmaids

Kitten Campout

by Sudipta Bardhan-Quallen

illustrations by Vivien Wu

A STEPPING STONE BOOK™
Random House 🏠 New York

Text copyright © 2021 by Sudipta Bardhan-Quallen
Cover art copyright © 2021 by Andrew Farley
Interior illustrations copyright © 2021 by Vivien Wu

Visit us on the Web!
rhcbooks.com

Educators and librarians, for a variety of teaching tools, visit us at
RHTeachersLibrarians.com

Library of Congress Cataloging-in-Publication Data
Names: Bardhan-Quallen, Sudipta, author. | Wu, Vivien, illustrator.
Title: Kitten campout / by Sudipta Bardhan-Quallen ;
illustrations by Vivien Wu.
Description: First edition. | New York : Random House, 2021. |
Series: Purrmaids ; #9 | "A Stepping Stone Book." | Audience: Ages 6–9. |
Summary: The purrmaids are going on their very first school sleepover, but Angel
feels left out when she is paired with Cascade, a member of the Catfish Club.
Identifiers: LCCN 2020006321 (print) | LCCN 2020006322 (ebook) |
ISBN 978-0-593-30163-0 (trade pbk.) | ISBN 978-0-593-30164-7 (lib. bdg.) |
ISBN 978-0-593-30165-4 (ebook)
Subjects: CYAC: Mermaids—Fiction. | Cats—Fiction. | Sleepovers—Fiction.
Classification: LCC PZ7.B25007 Kih 2021 (print) |
LCC PZ7.B25007 (ebook) | DDC [Fic]—dc23

Printed in the United States of America
10 9 8 7 6 5 4 3 2 1
First Edition

This book has been officially leveled by using
the F&P Text Level Gradient™ Leveling System.

To Elena,
a purr-fect friend

1

The morning bell had already rung. That meant sea school was in session! Angel was in her seat. But she wasn't sitting quietly at her desk. All she could think about was *leaving* sea school as soon as possible!

"It's finally the day of our sleepaway field trip," purred the teacher, Ms. Harbor. She grinned and twirled in the water.

Her earrings and tail rings shimmered in the light. "Are any of you nervous?"

"Yes!" answered the students. Well, most of them. Angel was shaking her head.

"I'm not nervous at all!" Angel said, laughing. "I can't wait to stay up all night!"

"You're always so brave, Angel," Ms. Harbor said. "For the rest of you, it is fine if you're feeling a bit nervous. I know that *I* feel like there's a whole school of butterfly fish swimming in my belly!"

"Me too," whispered a kitten with soft orange fur. It was Coral, one of Angel's best friends.

Angel leaned over to squeeze Coral's paw. "Don't worry, Coral. We'll be with you."

"That's right," added Shelly. She was

a kitten with silky white fur and Angel's
other best friend. "We stick together no
matter what!"

The three girls had been friends fur-
ever. They even wore matching friendship
bracelets. Every time they had an adven-
ture, the girls added a charm to remind
them of the good memory.

Angel, Shelly, and Coral were all in
Ms. Harbor's class this year. That made
school even more fun for Angel. She loved

learning with her favorite purrmaids in the ocean.

"I know everyone is excited to leave for Camp Sandcrab," Ms. Harbor said. "I purr-omise we will leave soon! For now, though, we have just enough time for one more lesson."

Some of the students groaned. But they all took out their notebooks.

"We're going to review what we've been learning about," Ms. Harbor said. She turned on the classroom shell-ivision. A picture came on the screen. "We've been learning about all the things we can see in the night sky."

Shelly raised her paw, then said, "Like the moon and the stars."

"There are also planets and meteors and comets," Coral added.

Ms. Harbor nodded. "What do we

call the study of all those things up in the sky?"

"I know!" Adrianna shouted. She was one of the girls in the Catfish Club. The other two were Umiko and Cascade. Sometimes, Angel and her friends didn't get along with the Catfish Club. But most of the time, all six purrmaids were good friends.

"Yes, Adrianna?" Ms. Harbor asked.

"It's called astrology," Adrianna answered.

Angel scowled. *That's not right,* she thought. But before she could raise her paw, Cascade yelled, "Actually, the study of things in the sky is called *astronomy.*"

"Cascade is correct," Ms. Harbor said.

Cascade smiled. But Adrianna looked down at the ocean floor. She seemed embarrassed.

Angel leaned toward Adrianna and whispered, "Don't worry—it's easy to mix up astronomy and astrology. Those words sound very similar." She winked. "I get them confused sometimes, too."

"We've been learning about *constellations*," Ms. Harbor continued. "Who can tell me what a constellation is?"

This time, Angel raised her paw before anyone else. "A constellation is a group of stars that draws a picture in the sky."

Ms. Harbor smiled. "Correct!" She clicked a button, and the picture on the shell-ivision changed. Now the screen showed two groups of bright stars. They were linked by lines that made each group look like spoons. "Which constellations are these?" she asked.

"Purr-sa Major!" Baker exclaimed.

"And Purr-sa Minor!" Taylor added.

"You're both right," Ms. Harbor purred. The shell-ivision showed pictures of other constellations. "We can try to find these constellations on our field trip. And I have a surprise for you. If we get really lucky today, we might be able to see something special. Have you ever heard of a shooting star?"

"I have!" Shelly shouted. "A shooting star looks like a star falling from the sky. But it's really a meteor."

Ms. Harbor nodded. "It's very rare to see a shooting star or a meteor. But tonight, we might see a lot of meteors."

"How?" Angel asked.

Ms. Harbor grinned. "Tonight is the Purr-seid meteor shower!"

Angel gasped. Seeing a meteor shower would be fin-credible! This was going to be a paw-some night!

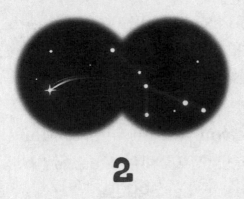

2

By the time the lunch bell rang, the students of Eel-Twelve couldn't stop talking about the meteor shower.

Angel always found it hard to float still. There were just too many things to do! Today, she ate her lunch more quickly than Shelly or Coral had ever seen.

"Slow down, Angel," Coral warned. "You're going to make yourself sick!"

"I can't slow down!" Angel exclaimed.

"I'm too excited! This is going to be the best field trip!"

Shelly nodded. "I think you're right," she said.

"Did you two bring everything on the packing list?" Coral asked. She pointed to a backpack that matched her soft orange fur. "I've double-checked my bag. But maybe I should check yours, too. I don't want us to forget anything important."

"Coral is always so worried about following the rules," Shelly whispered into Angel's ear. Coral usually tried to keep the girls out of trouble. It was one of the things Angel loved about her friend.

"Here's my bag," Angel purred. "I definitely packed my new octopus pajamas. But maybe you can check for everything else."

Coral started looking through it right

away. Angel held her paw in front of her mouth so Coral wouldn't see her smile.

Shelly placed her bag on the floor next to Coral. "Here's mine," she said. Then she grinned. "I can't believe we get to go camping. Overnight!"

"*I* can't believe we'll be hanging out at the surface of the water!" Angel exclaimed.

Purrmaids didn't go to the surface often. It wasn't always safe there. They spent most of their lives deep under the sea. In fact, there were lots of purrmaids in Kittentail Cove who'd never been to the surface!

Angel was lucky. She and her best friends had been to the surface a few times. The first time was when the girls visited Siren Island and saw narwhals. Another time was when Ms. Harbor took the class to Coastline Farm.

But today was even more special. The class wasn't just going to visit the surface. They were going to stay there for hours! Angel couldn't wait.

Coral didn't look excited, though. She looked a little nervous. "What's wrong, Coral?" Angel asked.

"There could be humans up there," Coral said.

Angel scratched her head. "My mother says that humans aren't dangerous as long as we leave them alone," she purred.

"I know that if we come across humans, we're supposed to stay away and give them plenty of space," Coral said. "But that doesn't mean they're not scary!"

"Coral," Shelly said, "Ms. Harbor told us that Camp Sandcrab is on an island hidden by rocks. Humans won't be able to find us."

"Besides," Angel added, "by the time we get to camp, it will almost be sunset. It would be too dark for humans to see anything."

"What about the moon?" Coral asked. "Won't there be a lot of moonlight?"

Angel shook her head. "We won't see

much of a moon tonight," she said. "I checked the calendar. It's almost time for a new moon."

"What happened to the old moon?" Shelly asked.

Angel giggled. "It's still the same moon!" she said. "It's just that the moon doesn't look the same all month. Sometimes, it's a big bright circle. That's called a full moon. Sometimes, it's a half circle, like the top part of a jellyfish. Then, during a new moon, you can't see any part of the moon at all. Which makes it hard for anything scary to see us." She grinned. "But it also makes it easier to see stars that are very far away!"

"That's why I picked this weekend for our trip!" Ms. Harbor purred as she swam over to the girls. "I should have explained it better before. I didn't mean for you to worry, Coral!"

"It's all right," Coral said. "Angel made me feel better."

Ms. Harbor patted Angel's shoulder. "That's what good friends do."

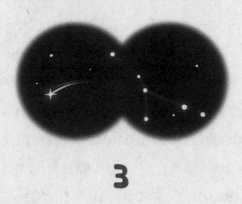

3

Before Ms. Harbor swam to the next group of students, she said, "I have to give you girls your bunk numbers."

Angel frowned. "I thought we were all going to be in the same place," she said.

"You are," Ms. Harbor said. "The bunks will all be lined up on the beach. But you won't all share the same bunk!"

"I hope not!" Shelly exclaimed. "I like having my own space."

Ms. Harbor smiled. "I do, too," she said. She checked her notebook. "Angel, you're in bunk seven. Shelly, you're in eight. And, Coral, you're in nine."

"Angel," Coral said, "you got lucky number seven."

"They are all nice bunks," Ms. Harbor said. "Number seven isn't luckier than number nine."

"I know," Coral mumbled. "It just *feels* luckier."

Angel bit her lip. "If it would make you feel better to have number seven, Coral, I'll trade with you."

Coral turned to Ms. Harbor. "Can we do that?"

Ms. Harbor nodded. "If that's what you girls want, I'm fine with it."

"That's really nice of you, Angel," Shelly said.

Angel grinned. "What are friends for?" she joked.

"You girls always make me proud by showing how kind you can be," Ms. Harbor purred. Then she winked. "Now I'm glad I have a surprise for you!"

"What is it?" Coral asked.

"Tell us, please!" Shelly added.

Ms. Harbor shook her head. "You'll have to wait until we get to camp!"

❀ ❀ ❀

It was finally time to leave sea school. Angel felt like it had taken fur-ever to be ready to go!

"We have a long trip ahead of us," Ms. Harbor said. "I would like you all to line up in order by your bunk number. That way, we can watch out for each other."

"I'm in bunk number one!" Baker announced. He floated to the classroom door.

"And I'm in two!" Taylor added. He floated behind Baker.

The other purrmaids lined up. Shelly was behind Coral. Angel was behind both of them.

Cascade lined up behind Angel. "I guess you're in bunk number ten," Angel said.

Cascade nodded. "Umiko is in bunk eleven, and Adrianna is in twelve," she purred.

"The six of us will be together again," Angel said.

"Actually," Cascade said, "the whole class will be together. Not just the six of us."

Angel sighed. "Of course, we will—" she began. But then Ms. Harbor asked for everyone's attention.

"I think we're ready, class!" Ms.

Harbor announced. "Shall we be on our way?"

Angel smiled. "That sounds purr-fect to me," she said. "I was ready to leave yesterday!"

"Actually," Cascade said, "if you left yesterday, you would have been too early to see the meteor shower."

This time, Angel had to force herself not to roll her eyes. Cascade was nice, but she could be a bit of a know-it-all.

Ms. Harbor had already opened the

classroom door, so Angel decided not to say anything to Cascade. She just swam closer to Shelly and Coral and whispered, "I'm glad the three of us will be together."

Coral and Shelly giggled. "Don't worry about Cascade," Coral whispered back. "You know she always has something to say."

"*Actually,* I did know that!" Angel joked.

The students of Eel-Twelve made their way through Kittentail Cove. Angel wanted to get to Camp Sandcrab as quickly as possible. Unfortunately, the camp was farther away than purrmaids usually go in a day. If Angel and her classmates had to swim all the way there, they wouldn't even reach the camp until morning!

Luckily, riding on the ocean current systems was a faster way to get around the sea. The purrmaids were planning to ride two different current systems to get from Kittentail Cove to Camp Sandcrab. First, they rode the Cross Cove Current to the Science Center, which was on the far edge of town. Then, they changed to the Western Catalina Current.

"We're almost there!" Ms. Harbor shouted as the purrmaids got off the Western Catalina Current.

But when the students looked around, they realized they were high above the ocean floor. "We can't camp here in the open water, can we?" Coral asked.

Angel shrugged. "I don't think so."

"Follow me," Ms. Harbor purred. She swam higher and closer to the surface of the ocean. The water got brighter as the purrmaids moved up. Before they knew it, their heads were poking out of the sea.

"Look at those!" Shelly exclaimed. She pointed at the ring of rocks around them. They stretched high into the sky.

"And look at that!" Coral added. She pointed to the beach of a small island tucked inside the circle of rocks. There was a sign that said CAMP SANDCRAB.

"We're here!" Angel shouted.

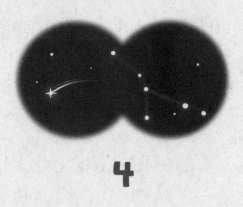

4

"Let's meet the camp director," Ms. Harbor said. She waved for the students to follow.

Angel swam the fastest toward the camp. But then something strange happened. Angel started to get stuck! "What's going on?" she asked. She looked around. Her friends were having trouble swimming, too!

Ms. Harbor was the only one who

was smiling. "You all need to stop flapping around!" she shouted. She sat down on the sand. "The water is really shallow here. We can't swim like we do in the open sea."

"Then what do we do?" Adrianna asked.

"Just sit down!" Ms. Harbor replied. "Use your paws to push or pull yourself around."

Angel did what their teacher suggested. Soon, she was sliding along the sand. "This is a lot easier!" she squealed.

"And fun!" Baker said.

"I could do this all day!" Taylor added.

"And you haven't even gotten all the way to Camp Sandcrab!" someone shouted. Angel saw a purrmaid sliding toward the class from the camp. She had the fluffiest gray fur Angel had ever seen.

Like Ms. Harbor, this purrmaid had rings in her ears. She was wearing a shirt that said CAMP DIRECTOR.

"Class," Ms. Harbor purred, "let me introduce you to Ms. Sanders."

"Welcome to Camp Sandcrab!" Ms. Sanders exclaimed. "I'm so excited to meet all of you! And I'm glad you're enjoying our wading beach."

Ms. Harbor smiled. "I hate to take you away from all this fun," she said, "but maybe we should put away your bags?"

"There's more to enjoy once you're not carrying all that stuff," Ms. Sanders said. "I will show you where we build sandcastles, and how to use our waterslide, and—"

"Slow down!" Ms. Harbor said,

laughing. "One thing at a time! Let's get my students to the camp."

Ms. Sanders led the way to one of the rock cliffs. There were shelves built into the rock. "You can drop your stuff off here for now," Ms. Sanders said.

The purrmaids plopped their bags down. Then Ms. Sanders waved for them to follow. "We're going to cook dinner at sunset," she said. "After you've eaten, we'll set up your bunks."

"And we'll get you ready to study the stars," Ms. Harbor added.

Ms. Sanders nodded. "But for now, you have a bit of time before the sun goes down to enjoy some camp activities." She pointed toward the cliffs. "That's a good spot for rock collecting." Next, she moved to a small raised area of sand that was surrounded by water. There were small shovels and molds of different shapes on the sand. "This is a sandbar," she explained. "We like to use it as our sandcastle zone."

"I've never built a sandcastle in the air before!" Angel exclaimed.

"Now is your chance!" Ms. Sanders replied. Then she led the class to a long rock that stretched from the sand into the ocean. "This is our waterslide," Ms. Sanders explained.

"How does it work?" Shelly asked.

"Climb onto it near the shore and lie on your belly," Ms. Sanders said. "Use your paws to pull yourself forward and then see what happens!"

"I'll go first," Ms. Harbor purred.

The purrmaids watched Ms. Harbor climb onto the slide. She lay down and pulled with her paws twice. She slowly moved down the slide. But when she pulled a third time, something changed. Ms. Harbor was suddenly boosted forward all the way down the slide into the deep, open ocean at the end. When she popped her head out of the water, she was grinning ear to ear. "That was just as much fun as I remembered!" she squealed.

"I want to go next!" Baker shouted.

"No, me!" Taylor replied.

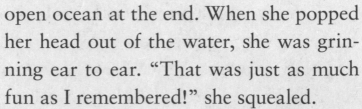

Angel turned to her friends. "I think there's going to be a line for the waterslide," she said. "Should we wait for a turn?"

Coral shrugged. "I don't know." She glanced at the

slide. "That might be a little too exciting for me."

Shelly put a paw around Coral's shoulders. "I would rather build a sandcastle," she purred. "Is that all right, Angel?"

Angel grinned. "As long as I'm with the two of you, I will be having fun!"

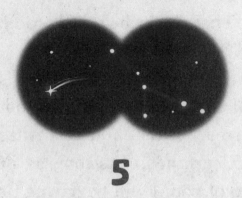

5

At the sandbar, the girls floated next to each other. The Catfish Club was across from them, working on their own sandcastle.

"How should we start?" Shelly asked.

Angel scratched her head. "I want to build a tall tower in the middle," she said. "Then we can build smaller towers all around it."

"That sounds good," Coral said.

"Actually," Cascade purred, "sand towers are wobbly. If it's too tall and thin, it won't stay up."

Angel frowned. "We'll be careful," she said. *I'm getting a little tired of Cascade,* she thought.

Cascade shrugged. All the purrmaids began working on their sandcastles. The Catfish Club had already built a big sand mound. Now they were using shovels to shape the sand.

Angel grabbed some molds and handed them out to Shelly and Coral. The molds were shaped like tubes. "Let's use these to build the tall tower," she suggested.

Angel went first. She used a shovel to fill her tube with sand. Then she placed it on the flat sand of the sandbar. She jiggled the tube gently. Then she carefully lifted it up. "Look!" she squealed. The sand left behind was the same shape as the mold.

"My turn," Shelly said. She repeated what Angel had done, except that she placed her mold on top of Angel's creation. Now the tower was twice as tall.

"Let me try," Coral said. She was more careful than her friends. When she was done, the tower was as tall as three molds.

"This is working just fine," Angel said. She filled her mold again and tried to add more sand to the top of their tower. But this time, something went wrong! When Angel lifted her mold off the sand, the whole tower wobbled. Then it fell down!

Angel frowned at the blob of sand left behind when her tower fell.

"Cascade tried to tell you that would happen," Adrianna said.

"Maybe we should try it their way," Coral said.

Angel clenched her paws. She didn't want to get upset in front of everyone. But it was so embarrassing! She didn't want to admit that Cascade was right.

Luckily, the sun was starting to go down. Ms. Harbor shouted for the class to gather. So Angel put her mold down and said, "We can do this later, I guess."

The girls scooted over to their teacher. She and Ms. Sanders were sitting in the water near the beach. Their tails were in the ocean, but their bodies were on land.

Angel tried not to look at Cascade. She didn't want to talk about the sandcastle. She sat down as far away from Cascade as she could.

"I'm sure you are all getting hungry," Ms. Harbor said.

"My stomach is growling," Baker said, nodding.

"I think that was my stomach, actually," added Taylor.

"Then it's good that it is time to make dinner," Ms. Sanders purred. She pointed to a bowl on the beach behind her.

"And we have a fin-tastic surprise for you!" Ms. Harbor added. She grinned and clasped her paws. "I've been waiting fur-ever to tell you! Ms. Sanders has planned a very special dinner for us. Something you can only have on land."

Angel remembered when their class visited Coastline Farm. They learned about different sea vegetables that were grown on land. "Are we going to eat sea cauli-flower? Or beach bananas?" she asked.

Ms. Sanders shook her head. "Those aren't camping foods." She lifted the cover off the bowl. Inside, there were some small, white things. "We're going to have roasted scallops."

Shelly scowled. "We eat scallops all the time, especially in my parents' restaurant."

"I bet you've never eaten scallops the

way we're going to make them tonight," Ms. Harbor said. She grinned. "Ms. Sanders has a very special way to cook them."

"We're going to roast them over a fire," Ms. Sanders announced.

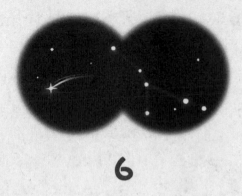

6

The class gasped. "Fire?" Umiko asked. "But you can't have a fire underwater."

"Actually," Cascade said, "we're not under the water right now."

"Exactly!" Ms. Sanders said.

"If any of you went rock collecting," Ms. Harbor said, "you might have found some special rocks." She held out her paws. She was holding a rock in each one.

"The rock on the left is called flint," she said. "The other one is pyrite."

"You can find these rocks near the cliffs at camp," Ms. Sanders said.

FLINT

PYRITE

"They're so sparkly," Angel whispered. "We should look for some before we go home."

Shelly and Coral nodded.

"While you were enjoying the camp," Ms. Sanders purred, "I gathered some of the things we will need. There's the flint and pyrite your teacher showed you. I also collected some twigs from the beach. I left them here in the sun so they'd get nice and dry."

"I helped Ms. Sanders dig a hole in the sand," Ms. Harbor said. "It's what humans call a firepit. This is where we will build our fire."

Coral raised her paw. "Excuse me," she said. She bit her lip. "Is it dangerous to make a fire?"

"That's a very good question," Ms. Sanders replied. "Kittens like you should never build a fire by yourselves. You always need a grown-up to make sure you stay safe."

"Ms. Sanders has a lot of experience with campfires," Ms. Harbor added. "It's a camp tradition!"

Ms. Sanders placed the twigs into the firepit. Then she took the two rocks from Ms. Harbor. She held them over the pile of twigs. Then she knocked them together. A bright spark came off the rocks and landed on the twigs. The purrmaids gasped as the twigs caught fire.

"Fin-credible!" Angel squealed.

"That was the easy part," Ms. Sanders said. "Now you have to cook your dinner." She picked up some long twigs and passed them around. "Everyone should stick a scallop on the end of their twig," she continued. "Then hold the scallop over the fire."

"The twigs are long enough that you won't accidentally burn your paws," Ms. Harbor said.

The purrmaids cooked their scallops over the fire. Angel was the first to taste the meal. She took a small bite.

"What do you think, Angel?" Shelly asked.

Angel grinned. "It's so good!" she exclaimed. "I want another!"

"These are too good to only have one," Coral joked.

"Or two!" Angel added. "I've already eaten four!"

"I'm so happy you like the roasted scallops," Ms. Sanders purred.

When the purrmaids were done eating, the sun was completely gone. The sky was dark blue. The first stars were starting to appear. But there were also a lot of clouds in the sky.

"Is it almost time for the meteor shower?" Adrianna asked.

Ms. Harbor shook her head. "We have to wait a little longer," she replied.

"Let's take this time to get you kittens set up in your beds for the night," Ms. Sanders said. "Can I have two volunteers to help me pull the bunks out onto the sand?"

"I want to help!" Baker shouted.

"Me too!" Taylor added.

"Purr-fect," Ms. Sanders said. "We'll call the rest of you over when we are ready."

Angel, Coral, and Shelly sat back on the sand and gazed up at the sky. "I wish it wasn't so cloudy," Coral said.

"I hope we'll still be able to find some constellations," Shelly purred.

Angel nodded. "It would be sad to come all the way up to Camp Sandcrab and have clouds get in the way of the stars!" She scanned the sky. Suddenly, she saw something. "Look there!" she cried. "I think I found the Crab!"

The Crab was a constellation of five stars. They made the shape of the letter Y in the sky. Angel pointed and said, "What do you think?"

Shelly and Coral followed Angel's paw. They both scowled. "I don't see it," Coral said.

"Me neither," Shelly added. "But maybe it's not dark enough."

"I really think it's the Crab," Angel said, frowning. But she didn't feel as sure as she had a moment ago.

The Catfish Club looked where Angel was pointing. Then Cascade said, "Actually, I think those are just stars. The stars

in the Crab make an upside-down letter Y in the sky. Those look like a right-side-up Y."

The other girls nodded. Angel looked at the sky again. Cascade was correct. The stars she saw made the right shape, but they didn't point in the right direction. She felt her cheeks turning red with embarrassment. *I keep making mistakes today,* she thought.

7

Umiko put a paw on Angel's shoulder. She whispered, "I really thought it was the Crab, too."

Angel knew Umiko was trying to make her feel better. But it wasn't working.

Just then, Ms. Harbor made an announcement. "Class," she purred, "I think we should get our bags. The bunks are almost ready."

The students headed for the rocks.

Angel was moving a little more slowly than usual. When she grabbed her bag from the shelves, she realized that Baker's and Taylor's bags were going to be left behind. "I have an idea," she said. "If Shelly can carry my bag, I'll grab these two. That way Baker and Taylor won't have to come back after helping with the bunks."

"That's so nice!" Coral said.

"I've finally had a good idea," Angel muttered. "It's about time." When she picked up the boys' bags, she knew she was doing the right thing. That made her feel a little better about the mistakes she'd made earlier.

When the students arrived at the beach, they

saw a line of giant clamshells set up on the sand. Ms. Sanders, Baker, and Taylor were pushing the clamshells open. "You can set up a sleeping bag inside each half shell," Ms. Sanders said. "These are close enough to the water that the waves will splash into them all night. Then you don't have to worry about your tails drying out!"

Angel remembered that Baker and Taylor were in bunks one and two. She guessed those would be the bunks on the far left. And she was right! Those were labeled ONE and TWO. She dropped their bags near those bunks.

That was when Angel realized something. Each clamshell opened up to make two beds. *But there are three of us*, Angel thought. *Shelly, Coral, and me. One of us is going to be sleeping alone!*

That was a big purr-oblem!

Angel spotted Coral and Shelly down the line of clamshells. She slowly swam past their bunks, numbers seven and eight. Her bag was already next to number nine.

"This is fin-tastic!" Shelly exclaimed. She fluffed her pillow and placed it on her bed. "I'm so excited!"

"Me too," Coral added. "I'm glad I listened to you. It isn't scary to be camping on land. It's really cool!"

"It's cool for you," Angel mumbled. "You guys get to be together."

"What are you talking about, Angel?" Coral asked. "You're next to us."

"Yes, but I'm not with you guys," Angel said. "You're both sharing a clamshell. I'm all the way over here by myself."

"It's just the way the numbers worked out," Shelly purred. "Clamshells only have two halves. Seven and eight have to go together. But nine isn't so far away!"

Coral frowned. "You're supposed to be in seven, though. You're only in nine because you traded with me." She gulped. "Do you want to trade back?"

Angel bit her lip. "I gave you that bunk so you wouldn't be as nervous," she said. "You'd feel worse if you didn't have the lucky number *and* you had to sleep by yourself." She sighed. "I can't take it back from you, Coral."

Coral looked relieved. She squeezed Angel's paw and said, "Thank you."

But then Shelly frowned. "You can trade with me, Angel," she said. "That way Coral isn't alone and neither are you."

Angel sighed. She wanted to say yes. But she was purr-ty sure her friend was just trying to be nice. *Shelly doesn't want to be by herself any more than I do*, Angel thought. She couldn't ask her friend to do something that would make her sad.

Angel shook her head. "I love that the

three of us always have each other," she purred. "It's just bad luck that clamshells don't come in threes the way best friends do!" She tried her best to smile. "You guys stay over in those bunks." She opened her bag and put her pillow into bunk number nine. "I'll sleep over here."

"Thank you, Angel!" Shelly exclaimed.

"You made that easy for all of us!" Coral said.

Angel's friends grinned and hugged her. Angel knew she should feel good about making them so happy. But there was a part of her that was disappointed. *I didn't know they'd just agree so quickly,* she thought.

"Let's get changed into our pajamas," Shelly said.

"Then we'll be ready to watch the meteor shower," Coral added.

Angel remembered her new octopus pajamas. She couldn't wait to show them to her friends! *Now I feel a little better,* she thought. She took them from her bag and said, "I'll race you! Last one to the changing rooms is a rotten skeg!"

8

Angel got to the changing area first. Adrianna was going into one of the rooms, and Cascade was going into the other.

"It'll just be a minute," Angel said. "Then it's my turn."

"Are you excited, Angel?" Coral teased.

"Yes!" Angel exclaimed. "I've been saving these pajamas for a special night."

Adrianna slipped out of the changing room. Angel rushed forward in a fin-stant.

She could hear the other girls giggle, but she didn't care.

Angel came out of the changing room with a huge grin on her face. Her pajamas looked even better than she'd imagined!

But as soon as she saw Cascade, her grin disappeared.

Cascade was wearing the *same* octopus pajamas!

Angel's jaw dropped. "I can't believe it!" she whined. "Cascade is wearing my pajamas!"

"Actually," Cascade said, "these are mine. We just bought the same ones."

Angel clenched her paws. Every time this field trip seemed like it might be getting better, something paw-ful happened. Now even her pajamas were disappointing!

Shelly put an arm around Angel's shoulders. "Don't be upset, Angel," she purred. "Your pajamas are still paw-some."

"In fact," Coral added, "if they weren't so paw-some, Cascade wouldn't have the same pair."

Angel knew her friends were just trying to help. But she didn't want any help right then! "I'm going back to my bunk," she said. "I just need to be alone for a bit."

Angel didn't wait for an answer. She swam away as quickly as she could, thinking, *I wish I could just go home!*

Back in bunk number nine, Angel pulled the blanket over her head. She didn't want to talk to anyone. She didn't even want to see anyone. And she definitely didn't want to stay up late. *The faster I fall asleep,* she thought, *the faster this trip will be over.*

Angel was startled when someone gently shook her shoulder. Cascade purred. "I brought you binoculars for tonight."

Angel frowned. "I wanted everyone to leave me alone," she muttered.

"I know," Cascade said. "I told the others not to bother you. Adrianna and

Umiko are back in their clamshell exploring with their binoculars. Shelly and Coral are doing the same thing."

Angel pushed the blanket off her head. She looked over at Coral and Shelly, and then at Umiko and Adrianna. It felt like they were far away—even though they weren't. In fact, as soon as Angel caught Shelly's eye, Shelly shouted, "Are you feeling better?"

"Did you get your binoculars?" Coral added.

Cascade handed them to Angel. She said, "Your friends wanted to bring you these. But I didn't have anywhere else to go. So I told them I would drop them off." Angel could hear Cascade take a deep breath.

"I'll leave, though, if you still want to be alone."

So far, Angel had built her sandcastle badly. She was wrong about the Crab constellation. She wasn't with her best friends like she wanted to be. And her special pajamas turned out to be less special than she thought. She didn't think she could feel any worse. But then she realized Cascade was trying to be nice. *Even though I haven't been very nice to her,* Angel thought. *And maybe she's feeling left out since she isn't with her friends, either.*

"Don't leave, Cascade," Angel said. "This is your clamshell, too."

Cascade smiled. She climbed into her bunk. "I really do think these are the coolest pajamas," she said. "But I wouldn't have brought them if I'd known it would make you feel bad."

Angel nodded. "It isn't your fault that I'm as grumpy as an eel," she said. "I'm just having bad luck with everything today." She sighed and lowered her eyes. "I've been looking forward to this field trip fur-ever. But now I just want to go home."

"Don't say that!" Cascade purred. "You've made this trip better in so many ways. You helped Coral feel less scared by giving her the bunk with the lucky number. You were brave enough to try the roasted scallops first. That made it easier for the rest of us. You remembered to bring Baker and Taylor their bags. That was very kind. And we haven't even gotten to the good part of the field trip yet. Don't you want to see the meteor shower?"

"I guess," Angel mumbled.

Cascade reached for Angel's paw. "If you weren't here, I'd be all alone."

Cascade managed to do something paw-some—she made Angel's frown turn upside down. Everything she said was so nice. Angel realized that no one could ever replace her best friends. But that didn't mean she couldn't enjoy things with other friends, too.

"I've been thinking about today in all the wrong ways," Angel said. "I should be more paw-sitive. Then I would have seen all the good things you saw." She reached out to hug Cascade. "Thank you," she whispered. "You're a good friend."

9

"Are you two coming?" someone said. It was Adrianna. "We're supposed to meet Ms. Harbor near the waterslide with our binoculars."

"We're going to be late," Shelly said.

"And you know I hate being late!" Coral added.

"Cascade and I were talking," Angel said. "We lost track of time."

"I'm not surprised," Coral muttered. Everyone giggled.

"Actually," Cascade said, "as long as we leave now, we will be on time."

The girls hurried to the waterslide. Ms. Harbor and the rest of the class were already there.

Lots of stars twinkled in the sky. But there were still a lot of clouds, too. "Hopefully, the clouds won't get in the way too much," Ms. Harbor said. "The Purr-seid meteor shower is supposed to start soon."

"How long will it last?" Umiko asked.

"The meteor shower will go on for a good part of the night," Ms. Harbor replied. "But first we have to find the meteors. Ms. Sanders told me they would appear in the northern part of the sky. Who knows how to spot the North Star?"

Immediately, Angel's paw shot up. "The North Star is the brightest star in the sky," she said.

Cascade slowly raised her paw. "Actually," she said, "the North Star is not the brightest star. It's only the forty-eighth brightest star we can see from here."

"She's right," Ms. Harbor said.

Angel felt her face grow warm. *I can't believe she embarrassed me like that!* Cascade didn't seem to notice, though.

"It's still a very bright star," Ms. Harbor continued. "Here's another hint. The North Star is part of Purr-sa Minor. That's a constellation of seven stars that looks like a scoop."

Angel looked into her binoculars. She scanned the sky. "There are so many clouds," she said, scowling. "It's not easy to see Purr-sa Minor."

"It's not easy to see *anything*," Cascade said.

Angel dropped her binoculars to try to find a part of the sky that wasn't so cloudy. She spotted a few. She checked them one by one.

Suddenly, Angel gasped. "I think I found it!" she exclaimed. "The North Star!"

"Where?" Cascade asked.

Angel pointed at a bright star in the sky. Cascade looked through her own binoculars and then grinned. "I think you're right!"

"Let's tell Ms. Harbor," Angel said. But when she turned toward her teacher, she saw that Ms. Harbor and the rest of the class were looking in the opposite direction.

"The North Star should be somewhere

in this part of the sky," the teacher purred, pointing.

Angel wondered, *Could I be wrong about the North Star?* She didn't think she was, but Ms. Harbor was the teacher. She probably knew better than a student would.

Cascade elbowed Angel and whispered, "You have to say something, Angel."

"I don't know," Angel replied. "I've been wrong a lot tonight."

"But you're not wrong now!" Cascade cried. She pointed at the rest of the class. "They're all looking south. We won't find the meteor shower over there."

Angel shook her head. "I think we should trust Ms. Harbor," she said. "It would be too embarrassing if I make another mistake."

"I haven't found the North Star yet," Ms. Harbor said, frowning.

Cascade scowled at Angel. "If you won't say something," she said, "I will!"

Before Angel could stop her, Cascade shouted, "Actually, I know where it is!"

"What did you say, Cascade?" Ms. Harbor asked.

"I said, I know where the North Star is," Cascade said. She pointed to the star Angel had found. "It's there!" she exclaimed.

All the purrmaids turned to follow Cascade's paw. Ms. Harbor raised her binoculars. After a moment, she put them down and grinned. "You're correct," she said. "That *is* the North Star. I had us pointed in the wrong direction. How did you find it?"

Angel couldn't believe it! *I finally got something right,* she thought. *And Cascade is going to get all the credit!* She felt her face growing warm again. She turned away from her classmates so they wouldn't see how upset she was.

Then Cascade said, "Actually, Angel is the one who found it."

10

Angel's eyes grew wide with surprise. She spun around to face Cascade. The other girl was smiling. "I told you to say something," Cascade whispered.

"I wasn't sure I was right," Angel replied. "I didn't want to make another mistake in front of everyone."

"Anyone can make a mistake, Angel," Ms. Harbor purred. "I just did! I looked for the North Star in the southern part of the sky!"

"If it wasn't for Angel, we would have missed the meteor shower," Cascade said. "We're lucky she's here!"

Angel blushed. "I'm lucky to have fin-tastic friends to help me when I need it," she replied. "But now it's time to stop talking. We don't want to miss the meteors!"

The purrmaids laughed. Then they raised their binoculars and looked toward the North Star. In a few moments, the first meteors appeared.

"Fin-credible," Angel purred softly.

"You know," Ms. Harbor said, "humans say that if you make a wish on a shooting star, it will come true."

Angel heard her classmates whispering about wishes. But she didn't say anything.

She smiled and thought, *I already have everything I could want.*

The purrmaids watched the meteor shower late into the night. They even took their binoculars back to their bunks. They wanted to see as many meteors as they could.

Angel didn't remember exactly when she fell asleep. It must have been during the Purr-seid meteor shower.

The sun was just poking up above the ocean. The tide was high. Angel yawned and looked around. Cascade was still fast asleep in the next bunk. A few steps away, Coral rubbed her eyes. Shelly stretched her paws. But they didn't look like they were going to get up yet.

Last night, the waves were barely able to splash into the clamshell bunks. Now the ocean was almost as high as the edges of the bunks. The shell was just about filled with water. It felt great! *Since everyone else is still sleeping,* Angel thought, *I'll close my eyes for a little while longer.* She settled back into her bed.

The next time Angel opened her eyes, the sun was shining brightly in the sky. She peeked over at Cascade's bunk. But it was empty!

Angel sat up and turned to find Coral and Shelly. But their bunks were empty, too. In fact, she was the only purrmaid left on the beach!

Ms. Harbor told everyone last night that they would go home right after breakfast. Angel wondered if she had slept too late. *Did I miss breakfast? Could they have left without me?*

Angel felt butterfly fish fluttering in her tummy. The trip to Camp Sandcrab started out really badly. She made a lot of embarrassing mistakes in front of everyone. But then she was the one who figured out where to find the meteor shower! *I thought all my bad luck was behind me,* she thought. But oversleeping and being left behind would be the biggest mistake of all!

Angel just wanted to find Ms. Sanders. *Hopefully, she can help me get home!* She was rushing so much, she swam right into Ms. Harbor and her classmates! "Oof!" the teacher moaned.

"Sorry!" Angel gasped. "I didn't see you! I thought you guys had left me behind!"

"We would never do that, Angel," Shelly purred.

"But when I woke up, there was no one here," Angel said.

"That's because we were planning a surprise!" Coral said.

"We wanted to thank you for finding the meteor shower last night," Umiko said.

"It was Cascade's idea," Adrianna said.

Cascade smiled. "Actually, I had two ideas." She waved to Ms. Sanders. "I remembered that you really liked the roasted scallops. So I asked Ms. Sanders to make more for breakfast."

"I think everyone was happy with that idea," Ms. Sanders said.

"Tell her about the second surprise," Ms. Harbor said.

Cascade nodded. "Coral and Shelly

remembered that you thought the pyrite was purr-ty," she continued. "So I found you some small pieces to add to your bracelet." She handed Angel four sparkly pieces of pyrite.

Angel didn't know what to say for a moment. She couldn't believe how nice everyone was being, especially Cascade. The trip had been filled with surprises. Some were definitely not fun surprises! But most of them were wonderful.

Angel turned to Shelly and Coral. "I can't add a purr-ty pyrite rock to my bracelet unless you guys have them, too," she purred. She gave them each a piece of pyrite.

"Thank you, Angel!" Shelly and Coral exclaimed.

Then Angel turned to Cascade. "I'd

like you to have a piece, too, Cascade," she said. "I hope it reminds you of this trip. You did a lot to make it fun for me."

Cascade's mouth hung open. She hugged Angel and said, "Thank you! I'm going to make this into a necklace. Every time I wear it, I'll think of you."

Angel smiled. "This was almost a purr-fect trip," she said.

"Almost?" Ms. Harbor asked.

Angel nodded. "We just need to do one thing to make it absolutely purr-fect," she said. She picked up a roasted scallop and plopped it into her mouth. "Let's eat!"

Swim into a new series!

Read on for a sneak peek!

Early one morning in Seadragon Bay, a young mermicorn named Sirena could not sleep. She pushed the curtain on her window aside. It was still dark outside! No one in the Cheval family would be awake yet.

Sirena fluffed her pillow. She pulled the blanket over her head. But she kept tossing and turning. *I'm too excited to sleep,* she thought. *What if today is the day?*

It was the first day of the season. For most mermicorns, that was just another day. But for all the colts and fillies in Seadragon Bay, it was a special day. That was when the Mermicorn Magic Academy invited new students to the school.

Magic was a part of mermicorn life. But like everything else, magic had to be learned. The best place for that was the Magic Academy. "I hope they pick me today!" Sirena whispered to herself. She finally gave up on sleeping. She floated out of bed and started to get dressed.

Sirena found her lucky blue top and put it on. She brushed out her long rainbow mane. She put on her favorite crystal earrings. Then she peeked out the window again. She could see some sunlight. *It's early,* she thought, *but maybe the mail is already here?*

Sirena swam toward the front door. She tried to be as quiet as a jellyfish. She didn't want to wake her family. But when she passed the kitchen, she saw that her parents were already up!

"Why are you awake?" Sirena asked.

Mom laughed. "Is that how you say good morning?"

Sirena sighed. "I'm sorry," she said. "I just wasn't expecting you. It's so early!" She swam to her parents and kissed their cheeks. "Good morning, Mom. Good morning, Dad."

"Good morning, Sirena," Dad neighed. "Are you hungry?"

Sirena nodded.

Dad started to put kelp pancakes on a plate. Mom floated over to Sirena. "So," Mom said, "today could be the day, right?"

Sirena nodded.

"That's why we're awake," Dad said.

"The day a colt or filly gets invited to join the Mermicorn Magic Academy is a big deal for parents," Mom added.

"I think a special day calls for a special breakfast," Dad said. His horn began to twinkle. Then a cloud of glitter floated toward the pancakes. There was a bright flash of light. Dad held out the plate. "What do you think?" Dad asked.

Sirena's eyes grew wide. "Smiley-face pancakes!" she exclaimed. "I love these!"

Sirena sat at the table. Mom floated over to sit across from her.

"Do you think they'll pick me today?" Sirena asked.

"I hope so," Dad said. "I've been seeing more and more of your sparkle."

"I've noticed it, too," Mom agreed.

All mermicorns had the power to use magic. And all mermicorn magic started with a sparkle of your horn. Her whole life, as soon as Sirena saw Mom's horn or Dad's horn twinkling, she knew something special would happen. Sometimes, it was a simple bit of magic, like adding a smiley face to her pancakes. Dad once made a rainbow appear underwater to decorate for her birthday party. Other times, it was something seriously awesome. Mom could create ocean currents to move their family quickly from one part of the ocean to another.

Sirena had been waiting to find her sparkle for a long time. Then, she'd be ready to learn magic. That meant she could stop going to regular school and start going to the Mermicorn Magic Academy.